silly Millies

The
15
Best Things
About Being
the
New Kid

Homework due Friday

Art at 1 PM

New kid today

Cynthia L. Copeland
Illustrated by Sharon Vargo

M Millbrook Press / Minneapolis

For Anya, who knows what it's like to be the new kid

–CLC

For Abby, the new kid in our family

–SV

Text copyright © 2007 by Cynthia L. Copeland
Illustrations copyright © 2007 by Millbrook Press, Inc.

Millbrook Press, Inc.
A division of Lerner Publishing Group
241 First Avenue North
Minneapolis, MN 55401 U.S.A.

Website address: www.lernerbooks.com

Library of Congress Cataloging-in-Publication Data

Copeland, Cynthia L.
  The 15 best things about being the new kid / by Cynthia L. Copeland ; illustrated by Sharon Hawkins Vargo.
     p. cm. — (Silly Millies)
  Summary: The new boy at school lists fifteen good things about being new, many of which relate to his having a fresh start.
  ISBN-13: 978-0-7613-2889-6 (lib. bdg. : alk. paper)
  ISBN-10: 0-7613-2889-0 (lib. bdg. : alk. paper)
  [1. Schools—Fiction. 2. Self-perception—Fiction. 3. Interpersonal relations—Fiction.] I. Title: Fifteen best things about being the new kid. II. Vargo, Sharon Hawkins, ill. III. Title. IV. Series.
  PZ7.C78793Aabf 2007
  [E]—dc22
                                                                        2005019498

Manufactured in the United States of America
1 2 3 4 5 6 – DP – 12 11 10 09 08 07

Being the new kid
is kind of scary.

Everyone stares at you.
Everyone asks you lots
of questions.

4

But being the new kid
is not ALL bad.
In fact, here are the

15 BEST THINGS

about being the new kid

1

Everyone thinks you are interesting.

2 The teachers will not come up to you on the first day and say,

3 No one knows that on the second day of kindergarten you used the GIRLS' bathroom by mistake.

You can run in the hall.

5 No one will tease you about bringing Bunny Car for sharing when you were six.

"... and I sleep with BUNNY CAR, and he goes to Grandma's house..."

The teachers will not tell you how much they liked having your big sister in class.

If you get sent to the principal's office, he will not say,

8 You can take a long time in the bathroom.

The nurse has not heard any of your excuses to get out of gym class when it is time for square dancing.

10 The lunch ladies do not know the tricks you use to get seconds on chicken nuggets.

11 No one has seen your
cool dragon shirt yet.

12

You can teach the kids new words.

13 The playground is new
and exciting.

"Awesome!"

24

25

You can tell the jokes that everyone from your old school knows, but no one from your new school does.

"What happened to the plant in math class?"

"It grew square roots."

"What did one math book say to the other?"

"I have a lot of problems."

"Why doesn't the math class need desks?"

"Because they have multiplication tables."

27

15 No one remembers when you brought in a rock for pet day.

Enjoy being the new kid while you can. As soon as another new kid moves into town, you turn into an old kid.

Tips for Discussion

- Are there things you did when you were younger that people still tease you about? What are they?

- If you were at a new school, what is the most important thing you would like the other kids to know about you?

- Do you have any new kids in your class this year? Do you think they like being new to your school?

- Do you have a brother or sister at your school? Do you like having the same teacher as your older brother or sister had?

- How do you think your younger brother or sister would like to have the same teacher as you had?

- What would you choose as your five best things about being the new kid?

About the Author

Cindy Copeland, who lives in New Hampshire, is the mother of three children and has written or illustrated more than 25 books. Her oldest child, Anya, was lucky enough to have been the new kid a few times and is now busy making new friends at college in Maine.